Gaensley

THE SEASHORE NOISY BOOK

By Margaret Wise Brown
pictures by Leonard Weisgard

HarperTrophy
A Division of HarperCollins*Publishers*

Muffin was a little dog with sharp ears. There was nothing he didn't hear. He could even hear the rain falling.

Muffin had heard the trucks roaring through the city and the birds whistling in the country. He thought he had heard everything.

But he had never heard the sea.

Then one day Muffin went to sea on a big sailboat.

Ho! Ho! said the Captain of the boat. *We'll make a little sailor out of Muffin.*

Muffin's nose tasted salty when he licked it. All around him was the sea. Wherever he looked as far as he could see there was cold water and a big sky.

Muffin could taste the sea.
Muffin could see the sea.
Muffin could feel the sea.
And he could smell the sea.
But could Muffin hear the sea?

Scree   Scree   Scree
What was that?
White birds were flying in the air.

And way off across the water he heard:
     Putt   Putt   putt   putt   putt
What was that?

Then a big ocean liner went by and blew
all its whistles.
How was that?

And a sailboat sailed by.
But could Muffin hear that?

Then slowly a gray wetness came in the air and Muffin couldn't see very far. What was that grayness?

Far off in the fog Muffin could hear:

Whoooo

Whoooo

Whoooo

Whoooo

What was that?

And he could hear:

lapping   slapping

slap   lap   lap

against the side of the boat.

What was that?

Then suddenly very close on the other side of the boat he heard:

D O N G   D O N G

d i n g   D O N G

D O N G

And from a nearby island he heard:

    Baaaa   Baa   Baaa

        What was that?

He heard:

    Toot   Toot

    Toot   Toot

        What was that?

And he heard a foghorn.

        How was that?

And then he heard a flutter of little birds' wings.

    sssswishshshshshshshshshsh

For when the big noises stop you can hear the little noises.

When the fog was gone and the sun was shining down on the sea, Muffin went ashore and walked along the beach.

First he found a jellyfish lying in the sand.
Could Muffin hear that?

Then he met a snail sliding down a rock.
Could Muffin hear that?

And in a pool under a rock Muffin found a starfish.
Could Muffin hear that?

Then Muffin found the big sea shell.
He sniffed all around it.
He pushed it with his paw.

Then he poked his nose inside the shell.
And that was when he heard the noise.
What was that soft low noise?

It was the sound of the sea.

Muffin was so busy listening to the noise in
the sea shell he did not hear the great
scuttling crab coming down the beach.

Then the crab scuttled up and nearly pinched Muffin's little foot. But Muffin grabbed the old crab by the back and threw him in the sea.

Then Muffin took a big drink of seawater. But he didn't like it. Why was that?

So he walked along in the warm soft sand. And he saw more crabs and pink shells and white shells and jellyfish and an old brown bottle.

At sundown Muffin heard the dinner bell. So he went back on the boat and they had crab soup for supper. Then it was night.

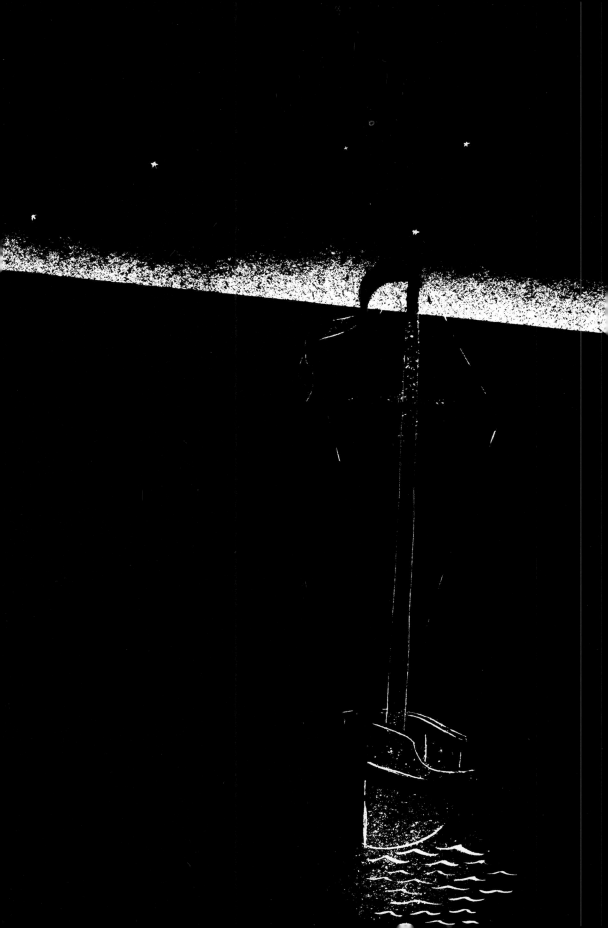

It was night and Muffin didn't hear a thing but the gentle lapping of waves around the boat.
The moon and the stars shone down on the sea. And you could see their light on the waters.
But could Muffin hear that?

The fish swam slowly about the sea.
But could Muffin hear that?

And lobsters crawled into lobster pots down
in the depths of the sea.
But could Muffin hear that?

And a giant shark swam round and round.
But could Muffin hear that?

And a swordfish.
But could Muffin hear that?

And some little tiny fish.
But could Muffin hear that?

And all around under the boat were
starfish and barnacles and flounders
and periwinkles and whales.
But could Muffin hear that?

Then in the morning they went fishing.
Flip flop the Captain caught a fish.
Flip flop flip flop it jumped on the
bottom of the boat. It was a mackerel!

Flip flop flip flop Muffin caught a fish.
Flip flop flip flop it jumped on the
bottom of the boat. It was a flounder!

Flip flop flip flop the Captain caught
another fish. It was a codfish!

Then all of a sudden there was a B I G
S P L A S H I N G in the water near the boat.
What could it be?

It was not a whale.

Was it the sun falling out of the sky?

N O

Was it a walrus blowing through his whiskers?

N O

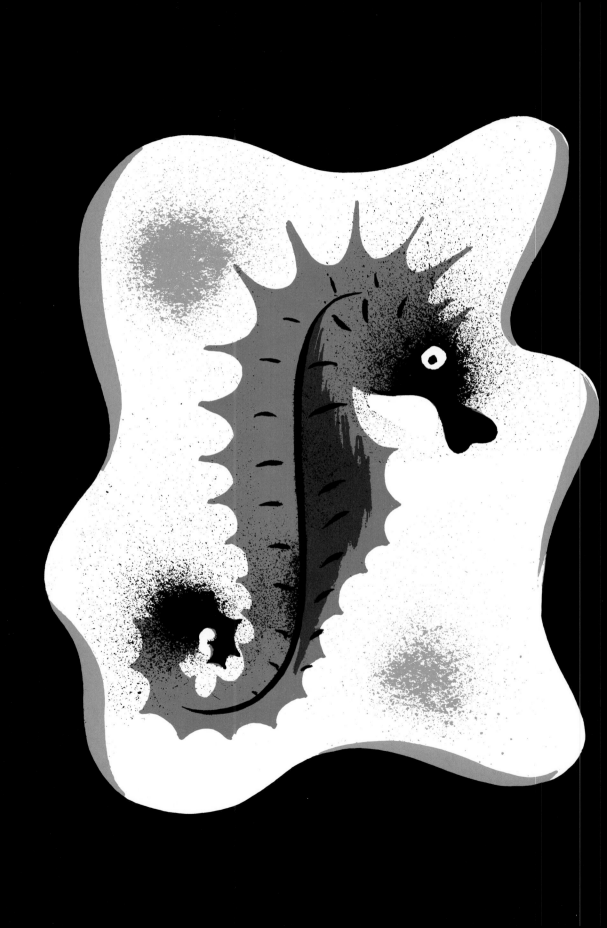

Was it a sea horse galloping?

NO

Was it a little shrimp?

N O

What do you think it was?

It was Muffin.

Swimming and splashing in the sea.

Ho! Ho! said the Captain as he pulled Muffin out of the water. *I think I've caught a dogfish this time.*